KU-165-751

HENRY

JAMES

PERCY

MEET ALL THESE FRIENDS IN BUZZ BOOKS:

Thomas the Tank Engine
The Animals of Farthing Wood
Biker Mice From Mars
James Bond Junior
Fireman Sam
Joshua Jones
Rupert
Babar

First published in Great Britain 1991
by Buzz Books, an imprint of Reed Children's Books
Michelin House, 81 Fulham Road, London SW3 6RB
and Auckland, Melbourne, Singapore and Toronto

Reprinted 1993 (twice)

Copyright © William Heinemann Limited 1991

All publishing rights: William Heinemann Limited.
All television and merchandising rights licensed by
William Heinemann Limited to Britt Allcroft (Thomas) Limited
exclusively, worldwide.

Photographs © Britt Allcroft (Thomas) Limited 1985, 1986
Photographs by David Mitton, Kenny McArthur and Terry Permane
for Britt Allcroft's production of Thomas the Tank
Engine and Friends

ISBN 1 85591 116 7

Printed in Italy by LEGO

DUCK
TAKES CHARGE

buzz books

"Do you know what?" asked Percy.

"What?" grunted Gordon.

"Do you know what?"

"Silly," said Gordon, crossly, "of course I don't know what, if you don't tell me what what is."

"The Fat Controller says that the work in the yard is too heavy for me," said Percy. "He's getting a bigger engine to help me."

"Rubbish!" said James. "Any engine could do it," he went on grandly. "If you worked more and chattered less, this yard would be a sweeter, a better, and a happier place."

Percy went off to fetch some coaches.

"That stupid old signal," he thought. He was remembering the time when he had misunderstood a signal and gone backwards instead of forwards.

"No one listens to me now. They think
I'm a silly little engine, and order me about.
I'll show them! I'll show them!" he puffed
as he ran about the yard. But he didn't
know how. By the end of the afternoon he
felt tired and unhappy.

He brought some of the coaches to the
station and stood puffing at the side of the
platform.

"Hello, Percy!" said the Fat Controller.

"You look tired."

"Yes, sir, I am, sir," said Percy. "I don't know if I'm standing on my dome or my wheels."

"You look the right way up to me," laughed the Fat Controller. "Cheer up! The new engine is bigger than you, and can probably do the work alone."

"Would you like to help to build my new harbour? Thomas and Toby are helping."

"Oh yes, sir. Thank you, sir," said Percy happily.

The new engine arrived next morning.
"What's your name?" asked the Fat
Controller kindly.

"Montague, sir. But I'm usually called 'Duck'," he replied. "They say I waddle." The engine smiled. "I don't really, sir, but I like 'Duck' better than Montague."

"Good!" said the Fat Controller. "Duck it shall be. Here Percy, show Duck round."

The two engines went off together. Soon they were very busy.

James, Gordon and Henry watched Duck quietly doing his work.

"He seems a simple sort of engine," they whispered. "We'll have some fun and order him about."

"Quaa-aa-aak! Quaa-aa-aak!" they wheezed as they passed him.

Smoke billowed everywhere. Percy was cross, but Duck took no notice.

"They'll get tired of it soon," he said. "Do they tell you to do things, Percy?"

"Yes they do!" answered Percy, crossly.

"Right," said Duck, "we'll soon stop *that* nonsense."

He whispered something to Percy and then said, "We'll do it later."

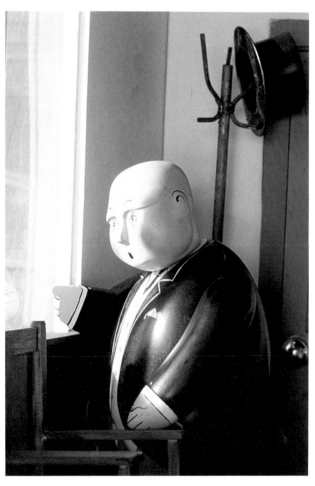

The Fat Controller had had a good day.
He was looking forward to hot buttered
toast for tea at home.

Suddenly he heard an extraordinary noise. "Bother!" he said, looking out of the window. He hurried to the yard.

Henry, Gordon and James were "wheeshing" and snorting furiously while Duck and Percy sat calmly on the points outside the shed, refusing to let the other engines in.

"STOP THAT NOISE," bellowed the Fat Controller.

"They won't let us in," hissed the big engines.

"Duck! Explain this behaviour," demanded the Fat Controller.

"Beg pardon, sir, but I'm a Great Western Engine. We do our work without fuss. But begging your pardon sir, Percy and I would be glad if you would inform these – er – engines that we only take orders from you."

  The big engines blew their whistles
loudly.
  "SILENCE!" snapped the Fat Controller.

"Percy and Duck," he said. "I am pleased with your work today; but *not* with your behaviour tonight. You have caused a disturbance."

Percy and Duck looked very worried.

Gordon, Henry and James sniggered.

"As for you," thundered the Fat Controller, "you've been worse. You made the disturbance! Duck is quite right. This is my railway and I give the orders."

Later Percy went away and Duck was left to manage alone. And he did so . . . easily!

THOMAS

EDWARD

GORDON